This edition published by Parragon Books Ltd
in November 2017 and distributed by

Parragon Inc.
440 Park Avenue South, 13th Floor
New York, NY 10016
www.parragon.com

Written by David Bedford
Illustrated by Brenna Vaughan and Henry St Leger
Edited by Laura Baker
Designed by Ailsa Cullen
Production by Rob Simenton

ISBN 978-1-5270-0974-5

Printed in China

I love my Grandpa

Parragon

Bath • New York • Cologne • Melbourne • Delhi
Hong Kong • Shenzhen • Singapore

One warm and sunny afternoon,
Little Bear went for a walk by the river
with Grandpa Bear.

"Should we go for a swim, Little Bear?"

Little Bear shook his head.
"I don't like water, Grandpa," he said.
"Let's just put one paw in," said Grandpa, "and see what it feels like."

Grandpa Bear put one
paw in the water.
"Ah!" he said.
"That feels good!"

Little Bear put only the tip of his paw in. Then he giggled. "The water tickles!" he said, and he put the rest of his paw in and waved it around.

"Wheeee!"

Grandpa Bear put
two paws in.

So did Little Bear.

Then Little Bear put all four of his little paws into the cool water.

"Good job, Little Bear!" said Grandpa.

"You're wading! Now, are you ready to make a splash?"

Little Bear kicked his feet,
making splashes with a

swoosh-swoosh-swoosh!

swoosh-swoosh-swoosh!

Then suddenly . . .

Splash!

In jumped Grandpa Bear,
showering Little Bear!

"Yippee!" cried Little Bear.

"Should we go for a swim now, Little Bear?"
said Grandpa.

Little Bear shook his head.
"I can't swim, Grandpa!" he said.

"Let's just float," said Grandpa,
"and see what it feels like. I will hold you."

When Little Bear felt his grandpa holding him,
he lifted up one paw at a time, until . . .

"You're floating!"
said Grandpa Bear.
"Now, how about some more splashing?"

Little Bear kicked his
feet, making more

swoosh-swooshes!

And suddenly . . .

"You're swimming,
Little Bear!" said Grandpa.

"Swim, Little Bear, swim!"

Little Bear swam around
and around his grandpa.

"You're the best little swimmer there is,"
said Grandpa Bear proudly.

When it was time to get out, Grandpa Bear helped Little Bear climb out of the water.

Then they both **wriggled** and **jiggled**
to get dry, spraying water all around.
"We're making a rainbow!" giggled Little Bear.

Grandpa Bear gave Little Bear
a warming hug.
"Do you like water now, Little
Bear?" he said, smiling.

Little Bear grinned. "I love water!"
he shouted happily. "And . . ."

"I love my grandpa!"

RIMONAH
of the
FLASHING SWORD

A North African Tale

adapted by
ERIC A. KIMMEL

illustrated by
OMAR RAYYAN

Holiday House / New York

AUTHOR'S NOTE

I came upon a traditional version of this story in *Miriam's Tambourine*, Howard Schwartz's collection of Jewish folktales from around the world. According to Schwartz, the story comes from Egypt. The idea of a North African Snow White intrigued me. I was also inspired by a comment of Jane Yolen's, that the heroines in older versions of traditional tales are far more dynamic than the Grimm brothers portray them. Elements of those older tales went into writing this story, as well as contemporary ideas about women's roles.

—Eric A. Kimmel

ILLUSTRATOR'S NOTE

Even though the story is Egyptian in origin, its timeless familiarity led me to place it not in Egypt, but in the more ambiguous world of folklore. Hence there are influences of ancient Egypt, Judaea, Persia, the Ottoman Empire, and Morocco.

—Omar Rayyan

To Trina and Barbara
E.A.K.

To Sheila and the flashing cats
O.R.

Text copyright © 1995 by Eric A. Kimmel
Illustrations copyright © 1995 by Omar Rayyan
Printed in the United States of America
First Edition

Library of Congress Cataloging-in-Publication Data
Kimmel, Eric A.
Rimonah of the Flashing Sword : a North African tale / adapted by
Eric A. Kimmel ; illustrated by Omar Rayyan. — 1st ed.
p.   cm.
Summary: A traditional Egyptian version of Snow White.
ISBN 0-8234-1093-5
[1. Fairy tales.   2. Folklore—Egypt.]   I. Rayyan, Omar, ill.
II. Title.
PZ8.K527Ri   1995   93-40091   CIP   AC
398.21—dc20
[E]

Once upon a time, beyond the sea, a queen sat by her palace window. She took a pomegranate from a basket. Sighing to herself, she said, "Would that I had a child with skin as dark as this pomegranate, eyes as bright as pomegranate seeds, and a voice as sweet as pomegranate juice."

Heaven heard her words. The good queen did have a child, a lovely daughter with skin as dark as a pomegranate's peel, eyes as bright as pomegranate seeds, and a voice as sweet as the juice of ripe pomegranates. The queen named her Rimonah, which means "Pomegranate."

Rimonah's parents, the king and queen, raised her with love and affection. She never knew the meaning of sorrow until the day she turned seven years old. On that day her mother died.

"Beloved Rimonah, I will always watch over you," the queen said. She pricked her finger and let three drops of blood fall into a crystal vial. "Wear this vial around your neck. The blood will dry in time. If it ever turns red and liquid, you will know that danger threatens." The queen closed her eyes for the last time.

After the queen died, the king vowed never to marry again. But there was a sorceress in the kingdom, a cunning beauty of boundless ambition, whose spells had caused the queen's death. She now plotted to win the crown for herself. She brought the king an enchanted cake. With one bite, he became bewitched and had no will of his own. He married the sorceress before Rimonah's mother was in her grave. The evil new queen's power spread like a weed, while that of the king withered.

Now, the queen possessed several magic treasures which she kept hidden in a tower room. Her favorite was a porcelain bowl. Whenever the queen filled the bowl with water, a face appeared that answered any question she asked it. One night the queen filled the magic bowl and asked, "Who is the fairest?"

The bowl had always replied, "Thou, O Queen, are the fairest in the land." But this night it gave a different answer. "Thou, O Queen, are fair, 'tis true, but dark-eyed Rimonah is lovelier than you."

Seething with jealousy, the queen ordered her huntsman to take Rimonah to the desert and kill her.

Rimonah suspected no danger, for the huntsman was her friend. She rode with him far into the desert. The huntsman suddenly drew his dagger. Rimonah cried out in surprise. Her mother's blood in the crystal vial around her neck turned liquid red.

"Do you mean to kill me?" she asked the huntsman.

"I must. The queen has ordered it," the huntsman said.

"Do not do this wicked deed," Rimonah pleaded. "Spare my life. Heaven will surely reward you."

The huntsman lowered his dagger. "Fly, Princess, while you can!"

Rimonah galloped away so fast she left her riding cloak behind. The huntsman killed a gazelle and soaked the cloak in the animal's blood. He brought it to the queen as proof that Rimonah was dead.

Rimonah's horse carried her to a bedouin encampment. The bedouin gave the child food and drink. After hearing her story, they said, "The free people of the desert fear neither kings nor queens. You may stay with us as long as you wish. We will protect you."

Years passed. Rimonah grew into a fearless young woman who rode with the reckless daring of a bedouin horseman. Her skill with dagger and sword was unsurpassed. Her fame spread among the bedouin tribes. Their chiefs brought gifts to her tent. Poets composed odes in her honor.